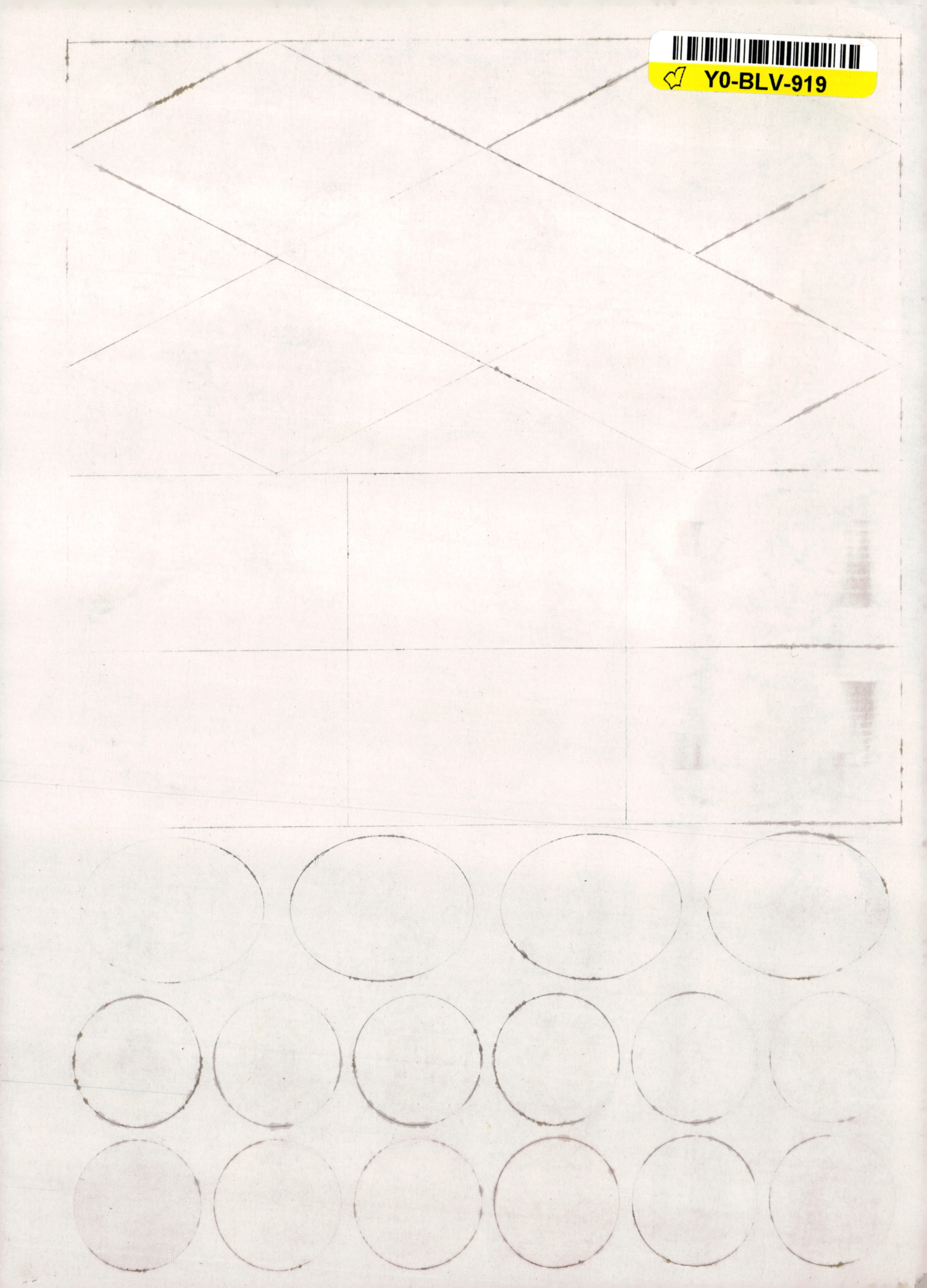

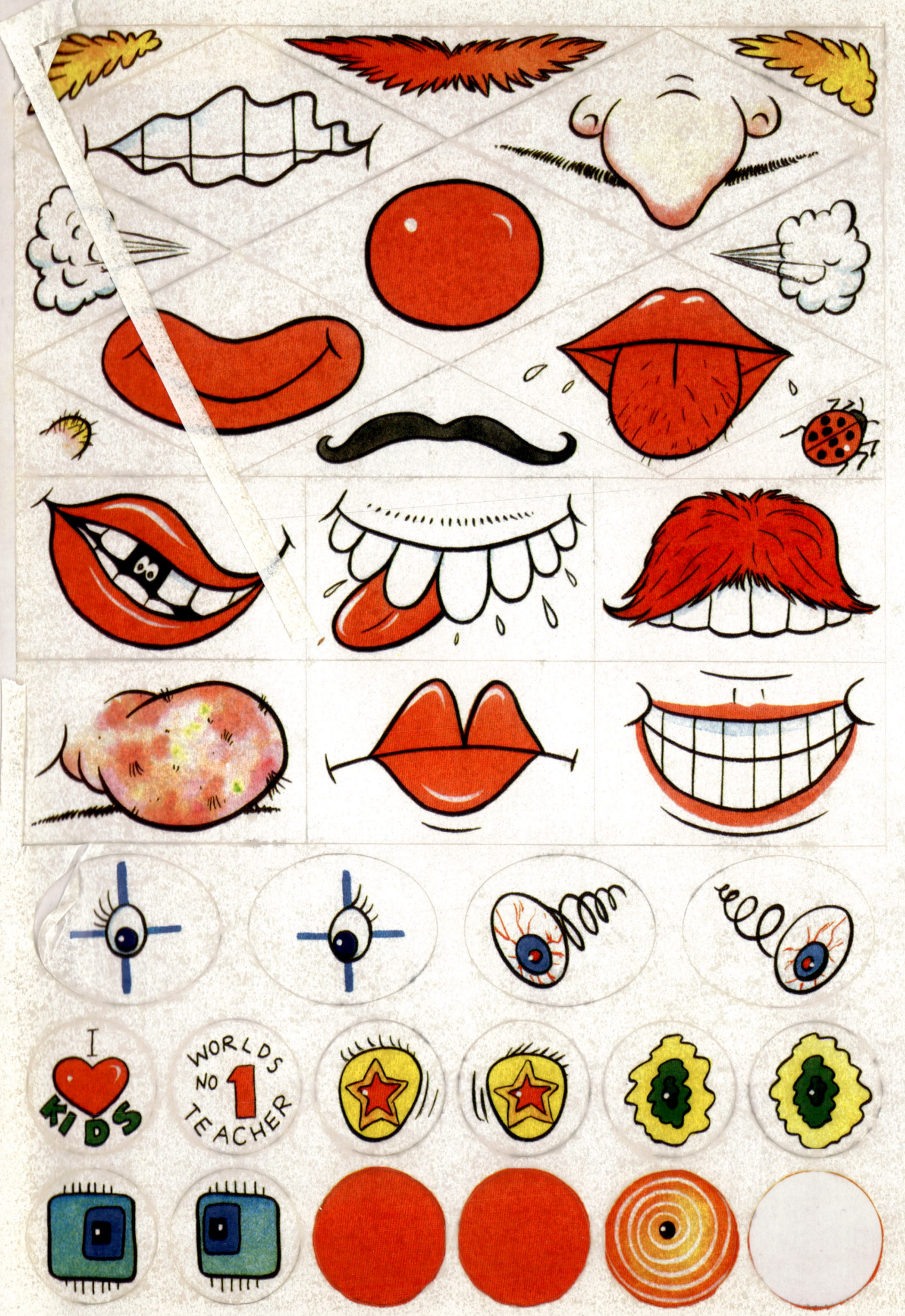

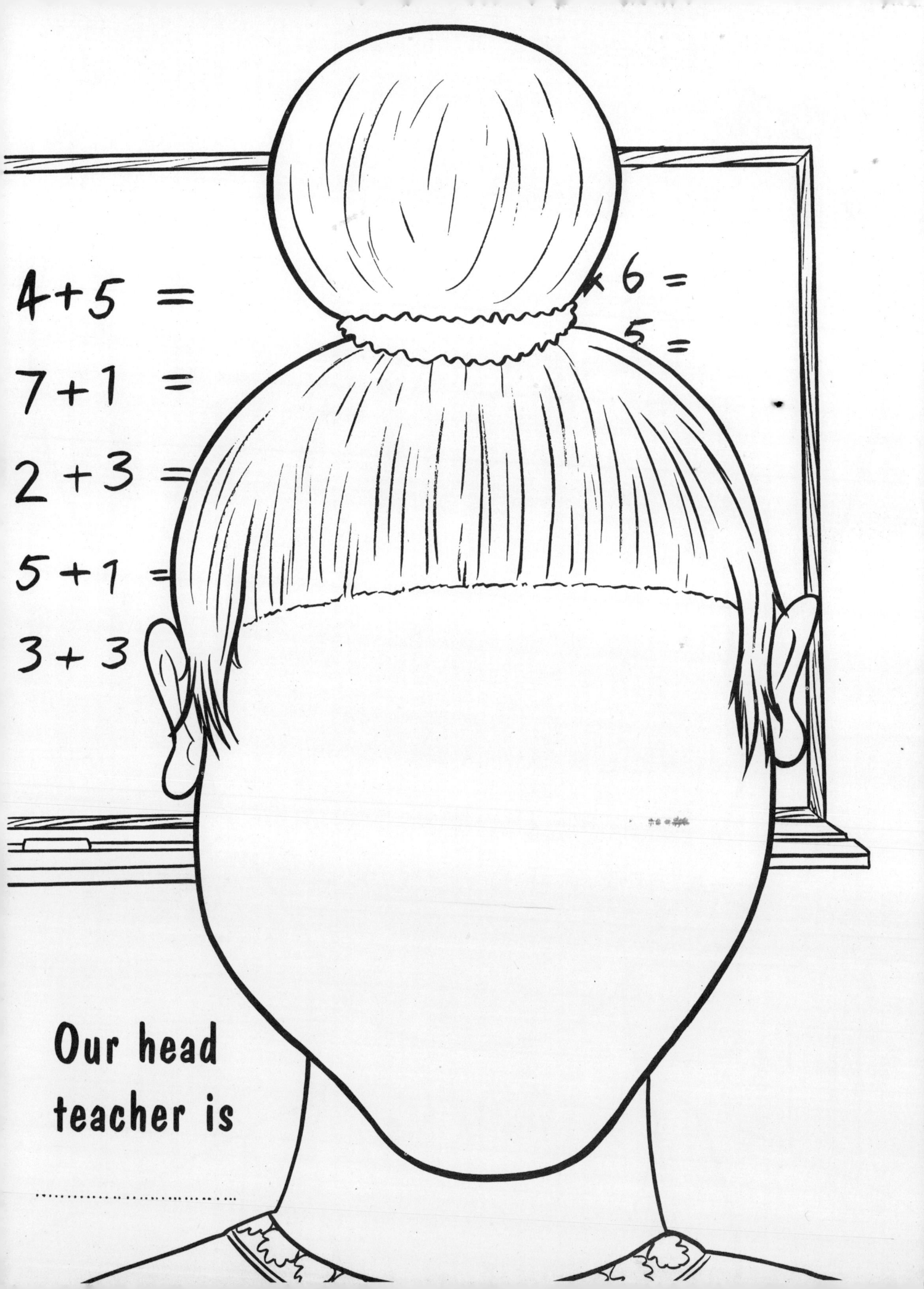

4 + 5 =

7 + 1 =

2 + 3 =

5 + 1 =

3 + 3

x 6 =

5 =

Our head teacher is

....

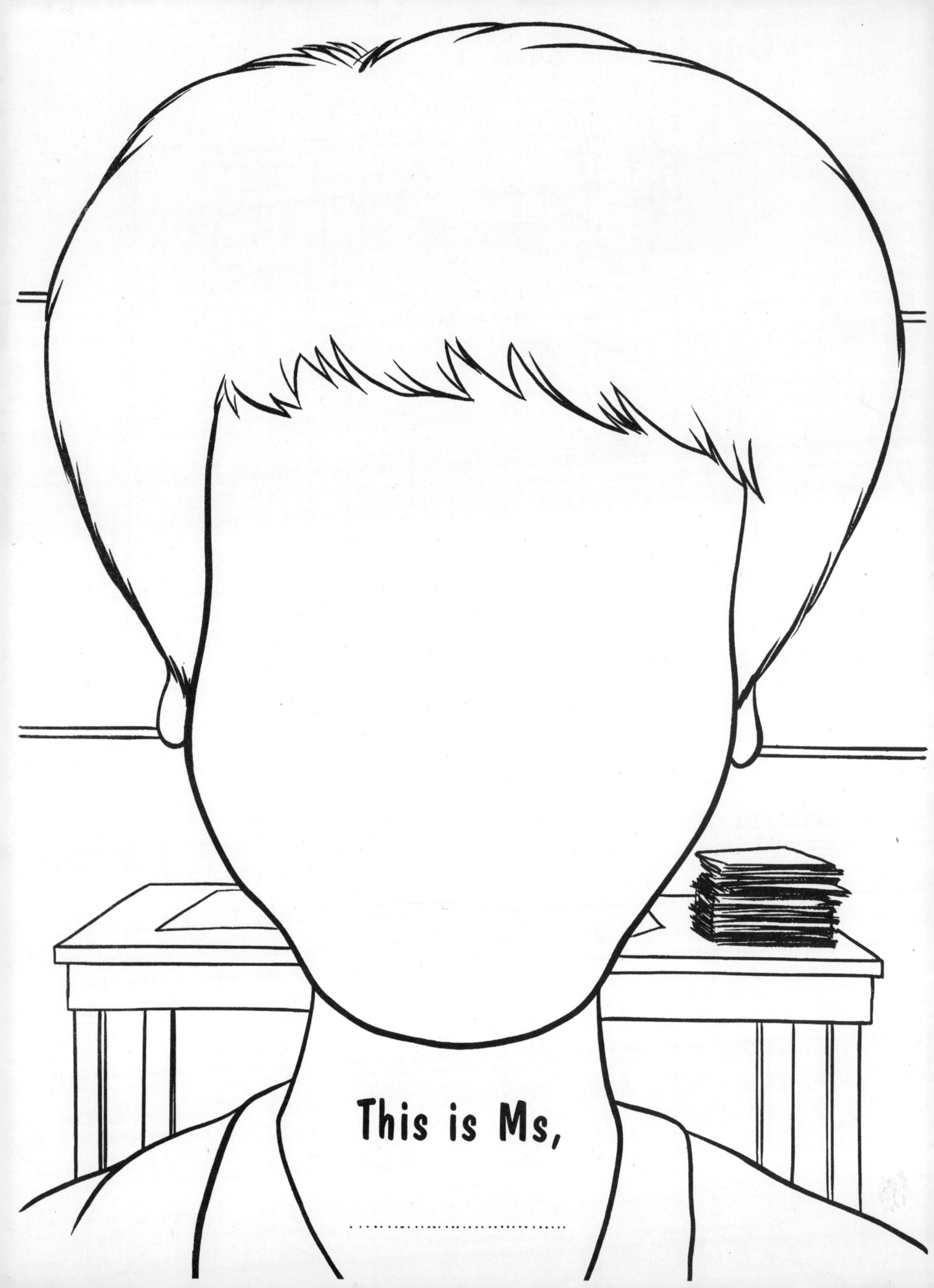

Our Lunch Lady is _____

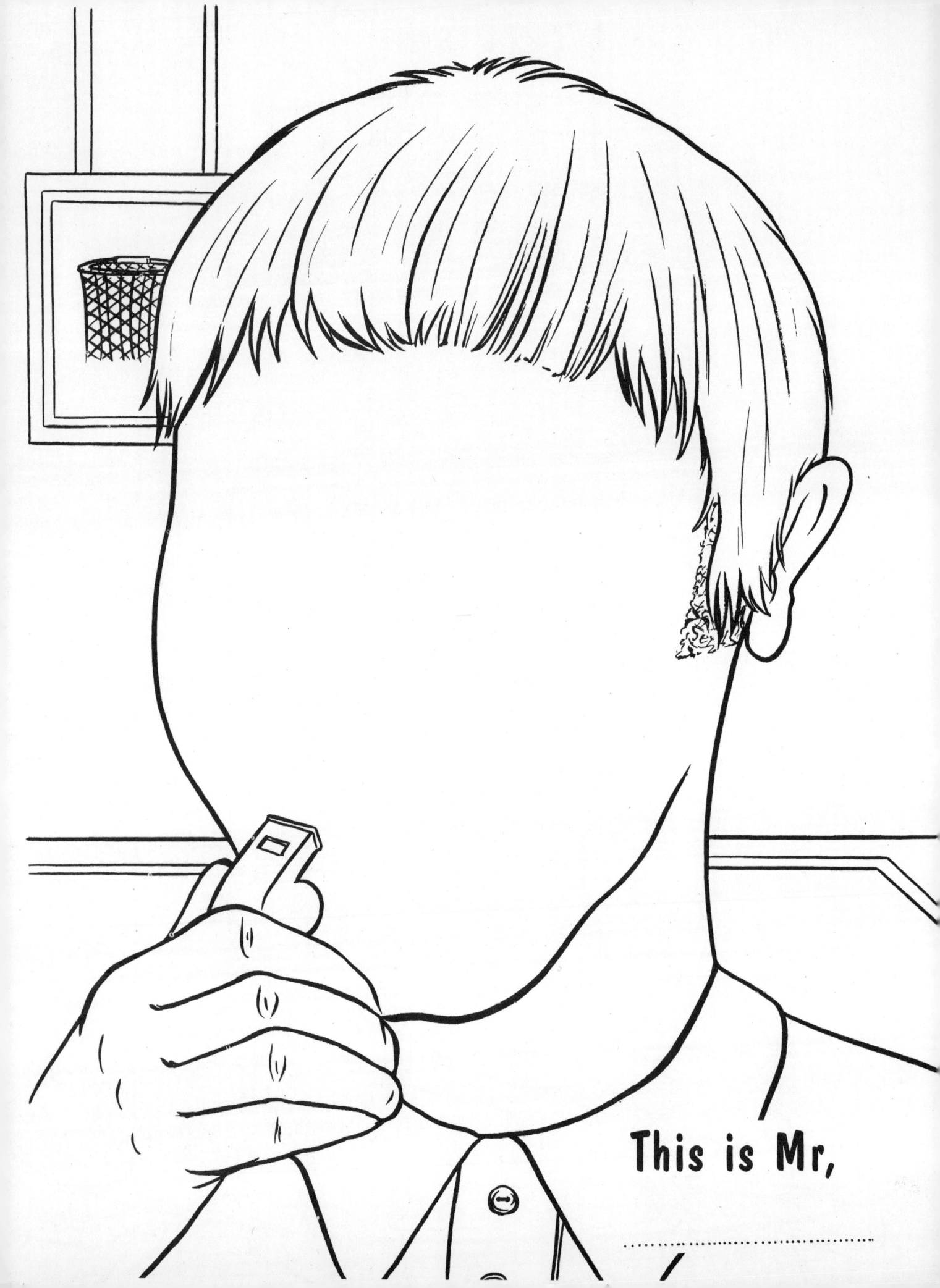

Our janitor is ....

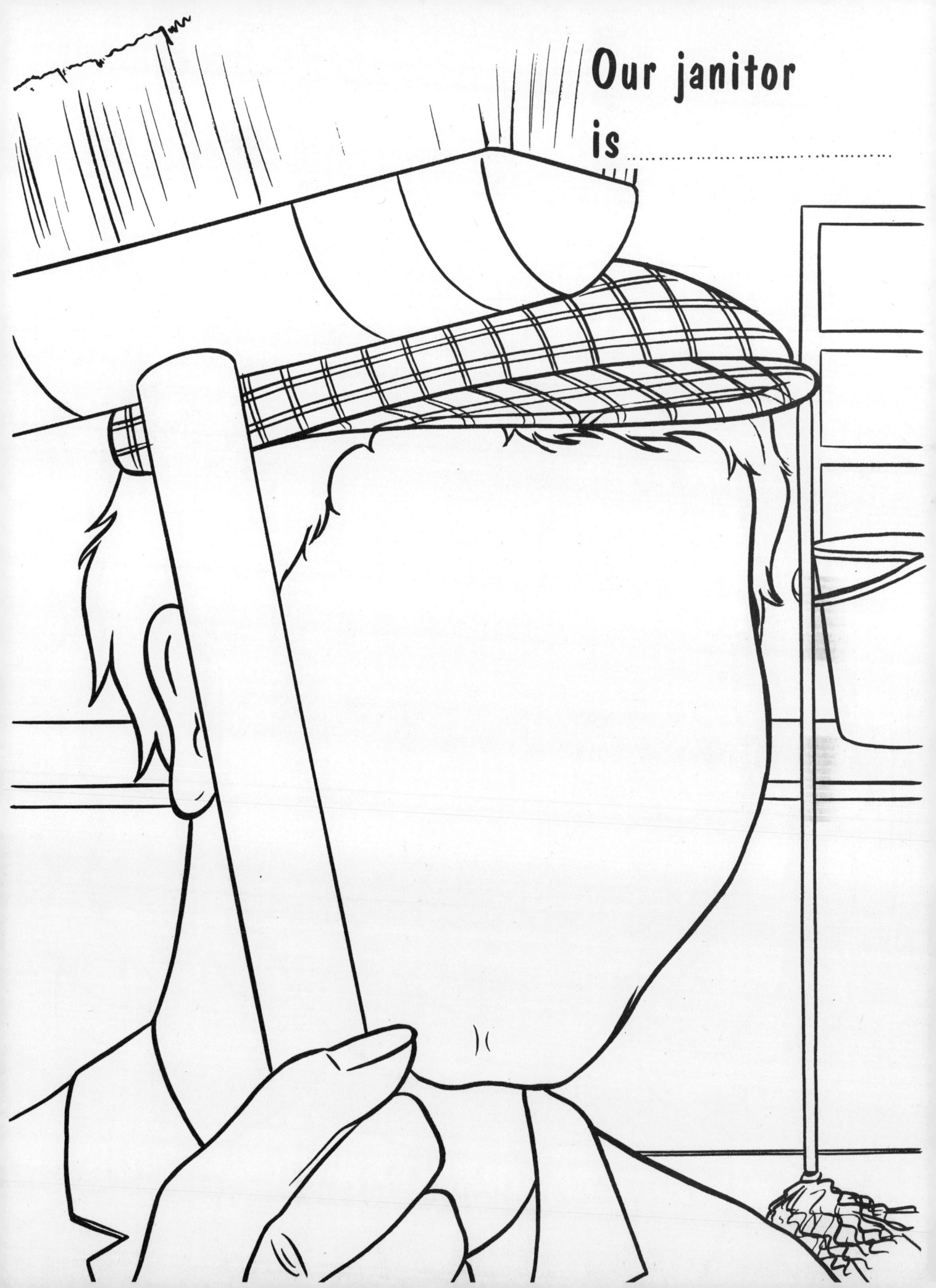

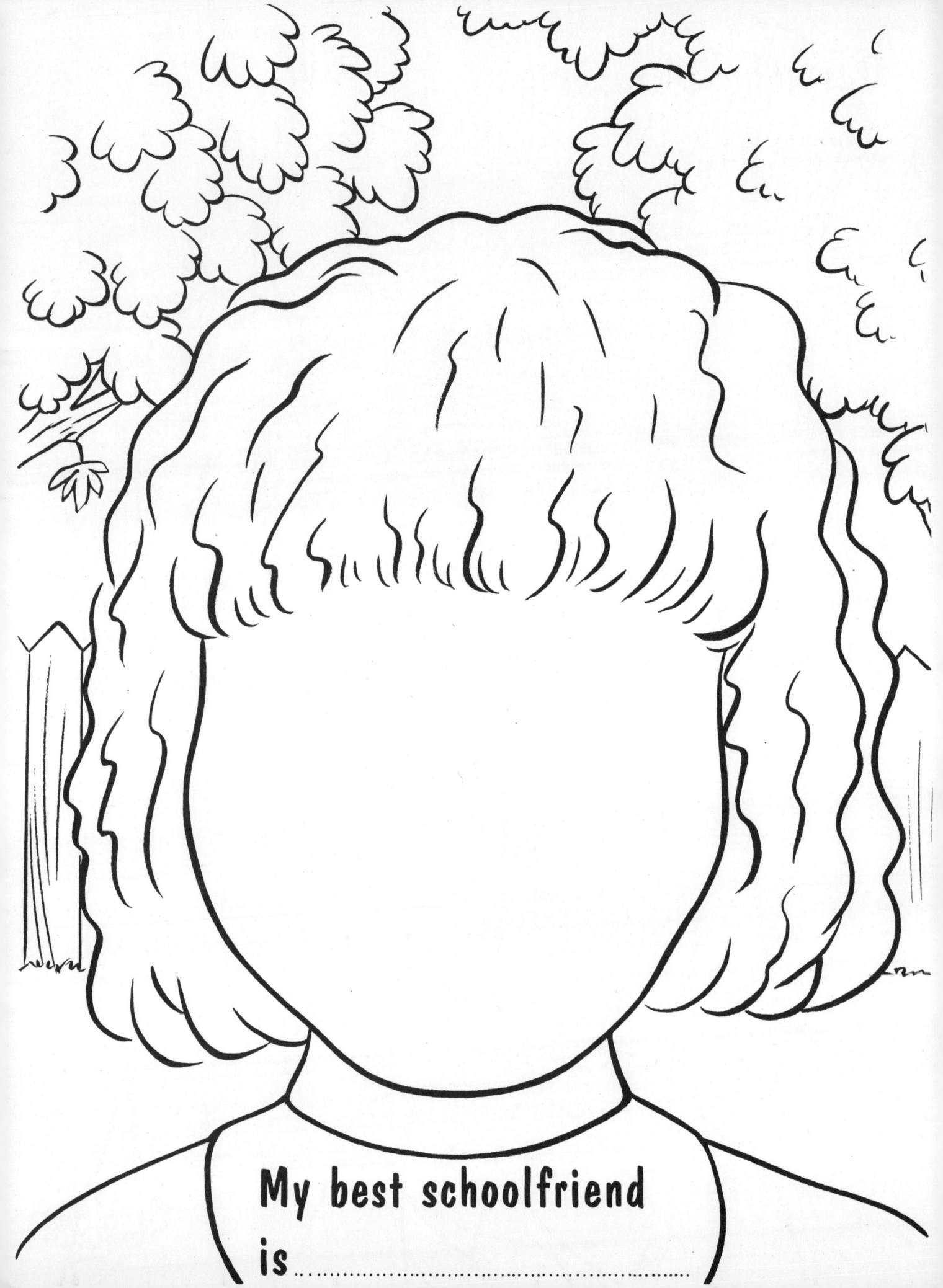

My best schoolfriend is..........

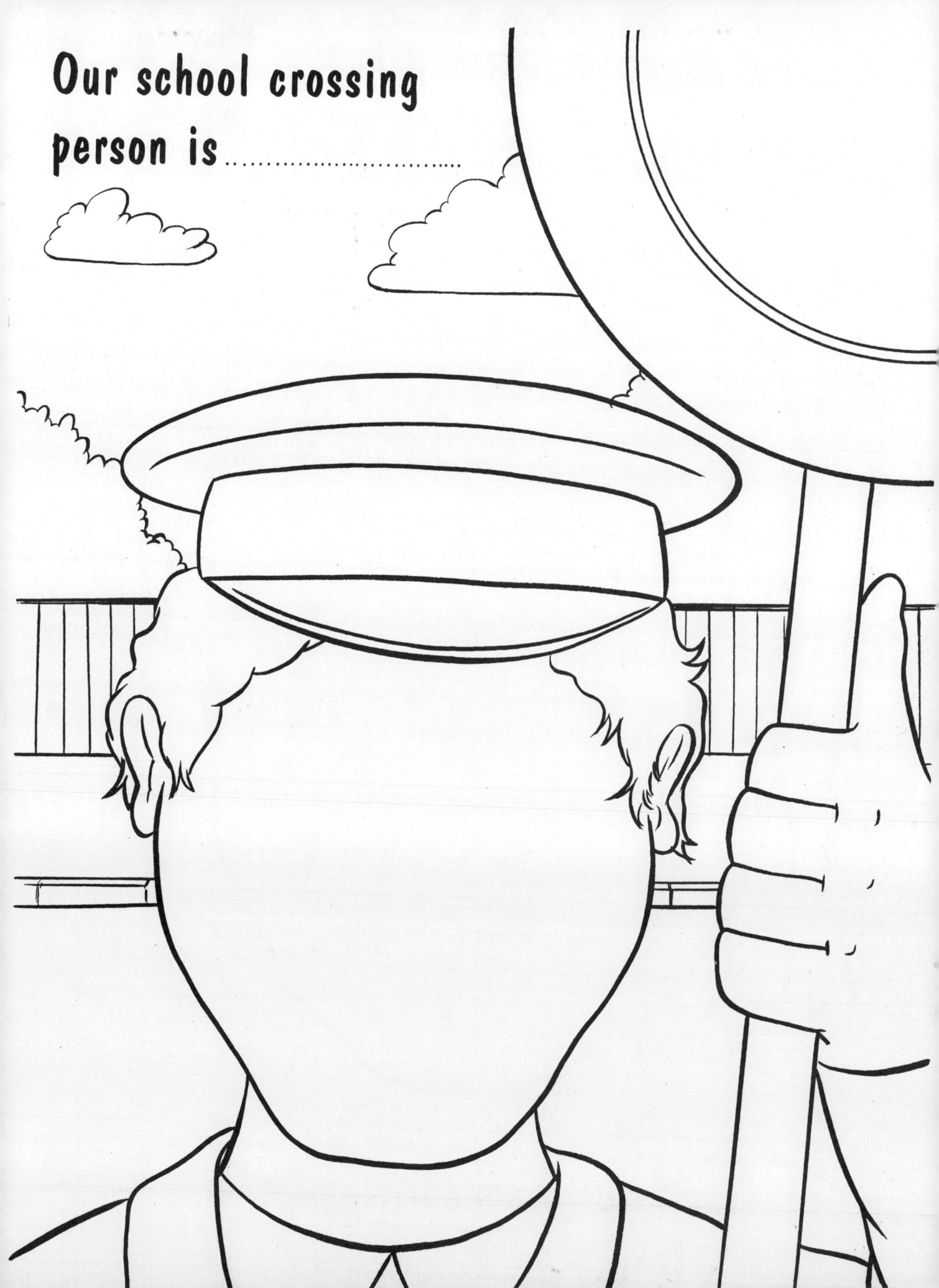

My best schoolfriend is ....

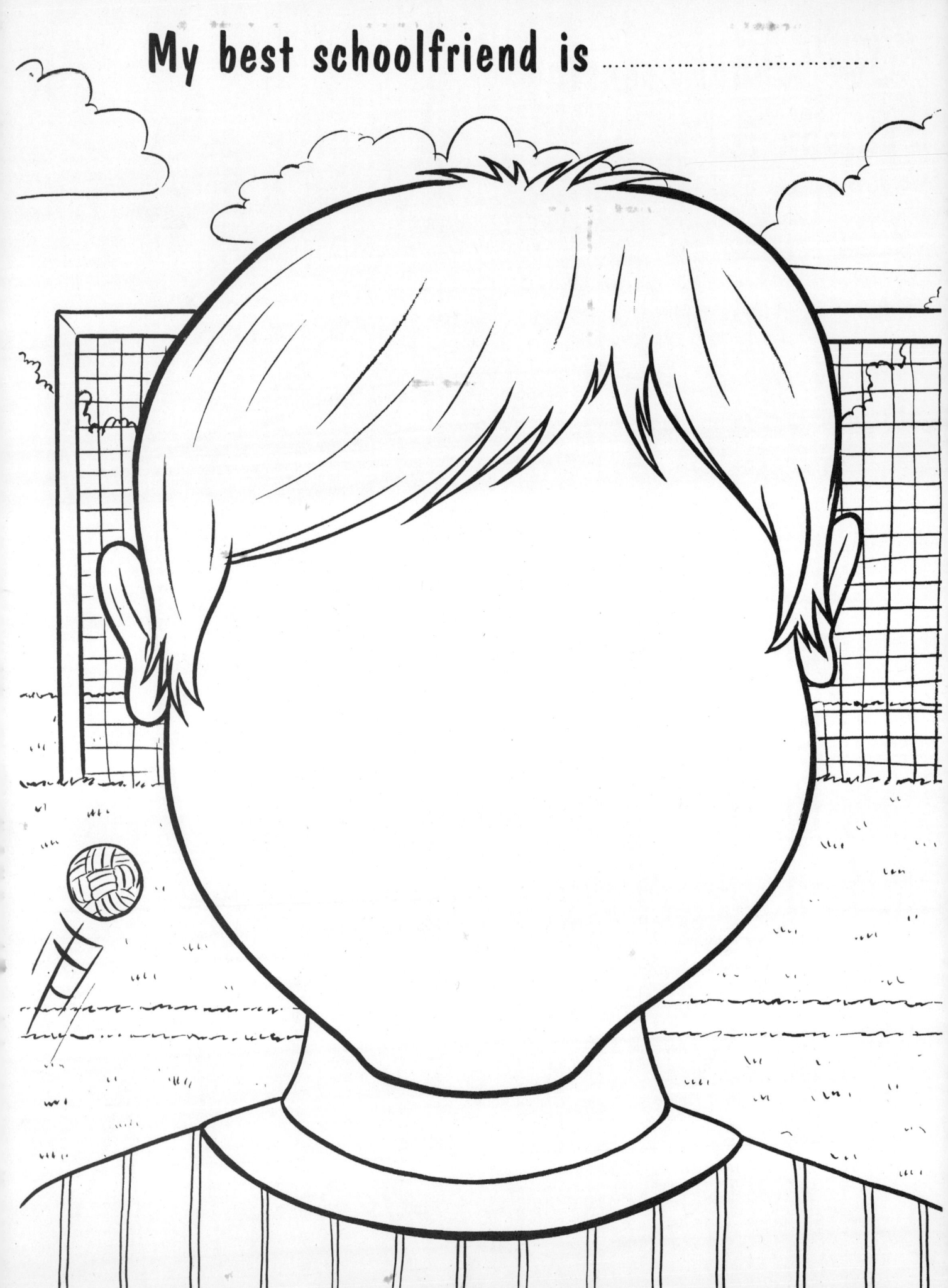